SNOUT ABOUT TOWN

STARRING

BUSTER KEATON BROWNE

A tale for precocious canines and their personal assistants.

Created by Petrine Day Mitchum

Drawings by Russell Jones • Color by Peggy Lindt

The authors are grateful to Ed Ruscha for permission to use an image of his painting *The Back of Hollywood* (detail), 1977, oil on canvas 22 x 80 inches, Copyright Ed Ruscha
Courtesy of the artist and Gagosian.

The authors are grateful for permission to use the following registered trademark: Logo for American Humane Hollywood's "No Animals Were Harmed" certification program. Use of the mark is not intended to certify any goods or services.

ISBN 978-0-692-93173-8

FOR

DOROTHY

Once upon a time,
in fact not very long ago at all,
a little brown puppy was wandering
the mean streets of Los Angeles.

He was alone, hungry, and scared.
What happened next was...
well, he wants to tell you
his story himself...

Hello! My name is Buster Keaton Browne. I am three–
in human years. There are no such things as "dog years."
Dogs just take longer to get through a year. I'm terribly
mature for my age.

I'm a Hollywood dog.

I was plucked from obscurity by the most fabulous movie
star, Lady B. By the way, that isn't her real name. Her real
name is a *secret*.

Lady B is very busy being famous so I have my own personal assistant.

Her name is Maggie.

Actually, Maggie is the one who discovered me, in prison!
I was just a puppy then...

Imagine *moi** in prison! It's hard to believe, but there are lots of excellent animals in prison right now! They didn't commit a crime–they are just homeless.

(*French for: *ME!*)

When Lady B adopted me, the paparazzi took our picture.
It was good for her image. Now we're both famous!

You don't have to be famous to rescue a furry friend,
but if you do, it will *definitely* be good for your image.
As far as I'm concerned, you will be a *star*!

We live in a condominium at the Famous Fabulous
Hollywood Towers. It's like a hotel, without the riff-raff.

Jason is my favorite doorman. He is teaching me French.
*Oui, Oui!**

(*French for: *Yes, Yes!*)

Everyone at the Towers is rich and famous, except Mrs. Guterman who is rich and famously grumpy.

Mrs. Guterman lives in the penthouse. On the elevator,
I quietly edge up to her and pass gas.

Mrs. Guterman's face turns red. I practice looking innocent.
I am a very good actor!

I have my very own room! Maggie is my roommate.

I'm her personal alarm clock!

16

Our house is the entire 17th floor.
On a clear day I can see the ocean.

My friend Shiloh lives in Malibu.

He has the biggest ears I've ever seen.

Someday we'll go surfing.

I was named for a famous clown who made silent movies in the olden days, before Lady B was even born and she's...well, I'm not allowed to say how old she is. It's in my contract.

That old Buster Keaton clown guy was very intelligent and athletic...like me!

I am not silent though.

I have many important announcements to make during the day.

Lady B gets *lots* of deliveries and it's my job to announce them.

I'm also an *excellent* singer. Maggie says I put the *wow* in *Bow Wow!!!*

Madame Crystal is my psychic advisor.

She says my ancestors were *excellent* rat hunters and retrievers.

Maybe I can retrieve Lady B's agent...

She says he's a real rat sometimes.

I didn't always believe in myself.

Dr. Sofa has taught me self-esteem. That's when you believe you can do whatever you dream. Mostly, I dream of eating.

Charlie is our chef. He is an *excellent* cook. Maggie is a *vegan*. It's our only bone of contention. I love bones! My favorite meal is steak on a bed of kibble with a dash of fish oil for my coat. *Bon Appétit!*

Charlie says I have a coat like a mink, which is a really cute little animal with shiny fur.

In the olden days, like when dinosaurs were in charge, some ladies wore coats made out of minks! *Yikes!*

If you aren't born wearing a fur coat, Lady B says fake fur
is the only way to go! It's cruelty free, plus it can be pink!
*Fabuleux!**

(*French for: *Fabulous!*)

In Hollywood, it's important to always look your best.
Accessories are *essential*.

I wear a different collar every day, depending on my mood.

Of course, staying in shape is *de rigueur**!

(*French for: *absolutely necessary!*)

I'm in charge of Maggie's fitness program.

In the morning we go to Beverly Hills.

I pick up messages from my friends.

I leave them some messages too.

Sometimes I add an exclamation point!

By the way, it's *de rigueur* to have an assistant who picks up your poop, especially in Beverly Hills where you can get a ticket otherwise.

Of course, biodegradable poop bags are the best. It's *extremely* important to take care of the environment, because where else would we live?

If it's a nice afternoon, which it usually is, we go to the dog park. Other dogs love to chase me. I'm very fast. Maggie says I am a *Tasmanian Devil!*

Keeping Maggie in shape is *beaucoup** work.

(*French for: *a lot of!*)

Later we stop at Le Chien Fou* Café. Maggie has a cappuccino.
I have a bowl of spring water and a peanut butter bone.

(*French for: *The Crazy Dog!*)

The shoe watching is *excellent*.

It's *essential* to have good taste in shoes.

Lady B loves an excuse to go shoe shopping!!!

Did I mention I'm terribly mature for my age?

Sometimes I
sneak up to the top
floor where Mrs. Guterman lives.

Maggie feels sorry for Mrs. Guterman because she is lonely.
I think she would stop being so grumpy if she had a dog
friend. There are plenty of homeless dogs who would be
happy to live in her penthouse!

Lady B says it's *essential* to be nice to others who aren't as lucky as you are, so Maggie and I deliver special meals –like Charlie's extra *fabuleux* spaghetti and meatballs– to people who don't have a cook.

I get lots of extra petting...and I might even get a meatball!

I am very lucky to have excellent health but sometimes I need a vaccination.

Dr. Hairball is my personal physician. He's got halitosis.* When it's time for the shot, I pretend I'm going to bite his finger and get a cookie to distract me.

(*fancy English for "stinko breath")

Afterwards we go for *sorbet*. It's ice, without the cream, and it's pink!!!

Lady B insists I get acupuncture to balance my *ch'i*, whatever that is. I prefer cheese and can balance it on my nose! Dr. Yang is very gentle–it doesn't hurt a bit!

Maggie thinks it's funny and calls me "Mr. Porcupine."

I love Maggie.

When Lady B is simply too tense from being famous, Uncle Paul makes a house call. He's not *really* my uncle but I let him pretend. His legs taste like coconut.

After her massage, Lady B *must* take a bubble bath and it's my turn with Uncle Paul. Massage is good for my circulation. *Très bien!*

(*French for: *very good!*)

Sometimes Lady B *absolutely* needs to "get away from it all" by riding her horse, Buttercup. I don't know why it's called "getting away from it all" because the paparazzi are always following us.

I usually find something delightful to roll in when Maggie isn't looking.

That makes Maggie *crazy* even though it's my hunting instinct to disguise my scent.

She calls me a "Royal Stink Rat" and shampoos me in the wash rack, which is like a car wash for horses. I'm worried that Maggie is developing O.C.D.D.*

(*Obsessive Clean Dog Disorder)

So much for my plans to hunt for dinner. It's Charlie's night off so we're having take-out.

Sometimes Lady B makes a movie on location, which means taking an airplane ride to someplace far from Hollywood.

Lady B has to learn her lines. Maggie and I do yoga so we don't freeze up. Charlie drinks a martini and takes a nap.

On location we stay in a hotel. It's *beaucoup* work to get everything ready so Lady B will feel at home. It's my job to make sure her bed is comfortable.

On the movie set, we have our own personal make-up artist. Lady B's make-up takes *hours* to apply. I never need make-up, but sometimes I wear a little fur gloss.

In Lady B's new movie, I made a cameo appearance. All I had to do was look cute. That part was easy, but we had to do the scene again and again because the actor kept forgetting his lines.

I almost passed out from dehydration. *Quelle horreur!**
Thank goodness there were nurses on the set.

(*French for: *The horror!*)

After I recovered, I showed the director my Tasmanian Devil dance so he'd know how versatile I am.

Next time I'm *sure* I'll get a barking role.

Maggie checks Lady B's email every night. I send doggie-mail to Shiloh. Here's how it works: I think of Shiloh and send him a picture with my mind. If he isn't busy, he answers right away.

Back in Hollywood, Maggie and I drive to Malibu with the top down.

Shiloh lives there with Maggie's boyfriend, Matt.

My favorite things about the beach are the sand and the ocean. Shiloh likes to bark at seagulls. Rolling in seaweed is *magnifique!** I love the beach!

(*French for: *magnificent!*)

After a day at the beach, Lady B says I smell like a dead fish. She *insists* I get a *proper* grooming.

First Maggie and I play hide and seek. I'm the hider.

Maggie is a very determined seeker.

When Maggie
is exhausted,
I give up and
we go to the
Euphuria Salon.

The hairdressers are very nice and give me lots of treats.
I still hate shampoo.

After my bath, Mrs. Guterman says I smell like a petunia and calls me "Boo-Boo."

I don't know what a petunia is but *je déteste** being called "Boo-Boo." That's a girly dog's name.

(*French for: *I detest!*)

It's a good thing I had my proper grooming because Lady B is nominated to win a Bald Guy Gold Statue! I don't see what the big deal is, but everyone in Hollywood wants one.

We have to get dressed up and go to a silly ceremony where everyone talks about how great they are. It's like the Westminster Dog Show, only for movie people.

All my fans have come to see me on the Red Carpet,
which is a special rug for famous movie people.

One of my fans dares to run onto the rug!
She's a hungry homeless dog!

When the paparazzi try to shoo her away, I growl at them until Lady B picks her up!

Lady B is a *real* star.

Maggie and I decide to skip the Gold Statue ceremony and take our new friend back to the Towers. It's her very first ride in a limo!

For once, someone besides me gets a bath.

Charlie makes us a special steak dinner and we watch the Gold Statue ceremony on TV. Lady B wins a Bald Guy and tells everyone they should rescue a dog!

We get lots of treats when Lady B comes home!!!

Later, Maggie takes us for our bedtime walk. Guess who is in the elevator? Mrs. Guterman must have realized her image needed improving because she has decided to adopt...Boo-Boo!

The paparazzi are waiting outside for us of course.

Now Mrs. Guterman and Boo-Boo are famous too!

Lady B takes us all shopping to celebrate!!!

Fabuleux!!! Très Bien!!! Magnifique!!!

We're the talk of the town!
Oui, Oui!!!

Petrine Day Mitchum is freelance writer, filmmaker and animal advocate. Her book, "Hollywood Hoofbeats, The Fascinating Story of Horses In Movies and Television," is now in its second printing (Fox Chapel). She was inspired to create "Snout About Town" by her longtime companion, Buster Keaton Browne, a brownish-black dog found as a puppy on a street in Burbank, California. Petrine lives with an assortment of rescued dogs and two horses in California's Santa Ynez Valley.
www.hollywoodhoofbeats.net
www.petrinedaymitchum.com

Russell Jones is an illustrator, cartoonist and saxophone-playing globetrotter residing in Shrewsbury, England. He has contributed to numerous books and publications in both the UK and international markets, including the self-penned humorous book entitled, "The Eat your Own Pet Cookbook." Although he does not have a pet of his own, he delights in his friends' dogs and was inspired by their many antics to create **www.cartoonadog.com.**

Peggy Lindt is a freelance commercial artist and illustrator living in Santa Barbara, California. Her wide range of work includes life-size fine art portraits of dogs.
www.peggylindt.com

The author would also like to thank: Jane Ayer, Joe La Corte, Frac Fox, Holly George-Warren, Eric Kelley & Gregory Simcoe for their help and endless cheerleading.